Mouse Paint

Ellen Stoll Walsh

 ORCHARD BOOKS

ORCHARD BOOKS
96 Leonard Street, London EC2A 4RH
Orchard Books Australia
14 Mars Road, Lane Cove, NSW 2066
ISBN 1 85213 179 9 (hardback)
ISBN 1 85213 571 9 (paperback)
Originally published in the USA by Harcourt Brace Jovanovich in 1989
First published in Great Britain 1989
First published in paperback 1991
This paperback edition first published 1997
Text and illustrations © Ellen Stoll Walsh 1989
A CIP catalogue record for this book is available from the British Library.
Printed in Belgium

This one's for my mom,
NELL ORUM STOLL-JONES

Once there were three white mice
on a piece of white paper.

The cat couldn't find them.

One day, while the cat was asleep,
the mice saw three jars of paint —

one red, one yellow, and one blue.

They thought it was Mouse Paint.
They climbed right in.

Then one was red, one was yellow,
and one was blue.

They dripped puddles of paint
onto the paper.

The puddles looked like fun.

The red mouse stepped into
a yellow puddle and did a little dance.

His red feet stirred
the yellow puddle until . . .

"Look," he cried.

"Red feet in a yellow puddle
make orange!"

The yellow mouse hopped
into a blue puddle.

His feet mixed and stirred
and stirred and mixed until . . .

"Look down," said the red mouse and the blue mouse.

"Yellow feet in a blue puddle make green."

Then the blue mouse jumped
into a red puddle.

He splashed and mixed
and danced until . . .

"Purple!" they all shouted.

"Blue feet in a red puddle
make purple!"

But the paint on their fur
got sticky and stiff.

So they washed themselves down
to a nice soft white

and painted the paper instead.
They painted one part red

and one part yellow

and one part blue.

They mixed red and yellow
to paint an orange part,

yellow and blue to paint a green part,

and blue and red to paint a purple part.

But they left some white
because of the cat.